BATMAN BEGINS™

training Bruce wayne

Adapted by Holly Kowitt
Screenplay by Christopher Nolan and David S. Goyer
Story by David S. Goyer
Photos courtesy of Warner Bros.
Batman created by Bob Kane

Designed by Rick DeMonico and Heather Barber

ISBN 0-439-74112-2

12 11 10 9 8 7 6 5 4 3 2 1   5 6 7 8 9/0
Printed in the U.S.A. First printing, June 2005

SCHOLASTIC INC.

New York   Toronto   London   Auckland   Sydney
Mexico City   New Delhi   Hong Kong   Buenos Aires

Bruce Wayne had been locked up in a prison in Bhutan. Every morning, the other prisoners attacked him.

The prison gruel always tasted terrible. "Can't they kill me *before* breakfast?" Bruce growled as he got ready to defend himself from a huge inmate.

After Bruce defeated the big guy, six other prisoners rushed him. They knocked Bruce into the mud. He bravely fought the convicts, flipping one prisoner into another.

"Solitary!" shouted a guard.

"Why?" Bruce demanded. "I don't need protection."

The guard pointed at the unconscious prisoners lying in the mud. "It's protection for *them*," he replied.

The guards tossed Bruce into a dank, dark cell and slammed the door behind him.

Bruce wasn't alone in the cell.

"My name is Ducard," a polite gentleman said from the shadows. "I speak for Rā's al Ghūl, a master warrior. He can offer you a path to your true purpose in life. When you are released tomorrow, pick a rare blue poppy from the eastern slope and carry it to the top of the mountain."

After a long search, Bruce found the blue poppy.

Bruce climbed up through sleet and ice to the monastery on the mountaintop. When he finally reached it, he was nearly frozen and exhausted from hunger.

Bruce entered the monastery and stumbled toward the throne of Rā's al Ghūl. Along the sides of the room, dozens of ninjas drew their swords.

"Wait," said Ducard. The ninjas backed off.

Bruce held out the blue poppy and Ducard took it for Rā's al Ghūl. Ducard translated the famous warrior's question: "Are you ready to master your own fear?"

"Ready?" asked Bruce, feeling confused. He
was shaking with weariness. "I can barely —"
Before Bruce could finish, Ducard kicked
him. "Death does not wait for you to be
ready," said Ducard. "Today, death is your
opponent. Facing death, you learn that you
are afraid . . . so what do you fear?"

Bruce remembered the terrifying time he had been attacked by bats in a dark cavern. Bruce also flashed back to the worst night of his life . . . when his parents were murdered by a mugger in an alley.

When Bruce felt stronger, Ducard showed him around the monastery. "Do you still think your parents' death was your fault?" asked Ducard.

"I feel more angry than guilty," Bruce answered.

Ducard showed Bruce a storeroom where a stack of explosives was kept. He tossed a pinch of powder, and a burst of smoky flame flared up. "Explosions can be used to distract and deceive," Ducard explained.

On a frozen lake, Ducard gave Bruce sword-fighting lessons. They circled each other on the ice. Ducard lunged with his sword, and Bruce blocked the blow with his silver gauntlet.

"Your parents' death was not your fault," said Ducard. "It was your father's. He failed to act."

"The mugger had a gun!" replied Bruce.

"Would that stop you?" asked Ducard. He leaped at Bruce.

Bruce knocked Ducard down and pointed his sword at his throat. "Yield," he said.

"You haven't beaten me," said Ducard. "While trying to defeat me, you gave up a safe place to stand." He tapped the ice beneath Bruce's feet.

The ice cracked, and Bruce plunged into the freezing water.

After many months of lessons, Bruce was tested in the monastery's training room. He had to stand on narrow poles while ninjas attacked him with long staves.

It was a tough battle, but in the end, Bruce defeated all the other ninjas.

Ducard was impressed with Bruce's skills. "You're ready," he said proudly.

In the throne room, Ducard
ground up Bruce's blue poppy. He
poured the dust onto the altar's
candles so Bruce could breathe in
the dizzying smoke.

"Face your fears," Ducard said,
and they both put on ninja masks.

Ninjas stepped out of the shadows.
Ducard vanished, blending into the crowd.
"To conquer fear, you must become fear,"
Bruce heard him say, "and men fear most
what they cannot see."

Bruce spun around quickly, but Ducard had disappeared.

Then Ducard stepped out from the rows of masked ninjas. He slashed Bruce's sleeve with his sword before vanishing again.

Some of the ninjas shifted aside, revealing a wooden box behind them.

Bruce approached the box slowly. . . .

Bats burst out of the box.

Bruce struggled to control his fear while the ninjas attacked from all sides. Bruce sliced a few ninjas' sleeves.

Ducard knocked down one ninja who had a slashed sleeve. He held his sword to the ninja's neck. "Become one with the darkness," he said, "and do not leave any sign."

"I haven't," Bruce replied. He was actually standing behind Ducard, his own sword pointing at Ducard's neck.

Ducard smiled.

Ducard led Bruce over to Rā's al Ghūl, where Bruce was given a burning candle and a cup. "We have purged your fear," Ducard translated for Rā's al Ghūl. "You will lead these ninjas. You are ready to become a member of the League of Shadows. Drink."

"By blowing out this candle you give up your life," Ducard continued. "You will help us destroy the city of Gotham. When it falls, other cities will follow."

Bruce did not blow out the candle. "You can't believe in this," he said.

"Rā's al Ghūl rescued you," Ducard replied. "In return, you must do what is necessary."

Bruce tipped over the candle with his
sword. Flames spread across the floor.

"What are you doing?" demanded Ducard.

"What is necessary," Bruce replied. With
his sword hilt, he struck Ducard on the head,
knocking him out. Then Bruce lit his mask
on fire and tossed it into the storeroom where
the gunpowder was kept.

Thunderous blasts filled the hall.

Rā's al Ghūl leaped off his throne, striking at Bruce with his sword. Bruce fought back, parrying the master's blows.

Bruce had never fought a more skilled opponent. Rā's al Ghūl was frighteningly swift and strong.

More explosions roared
from the balcony. Flames
swirled across the room
as Bruce and Rā's al Ghūl
battled in the training area.
Bruce fought his fear
and did not allow himself
to think about defeat.

The fire had weakened the ceiling. It collapsed.

Bruce jumped clear as flaming debris toppled down onto Rā's al Ghūl, crushing the master warrior.

Ducard was still unconscious on the floor. Bruce dragged him out of the throne room. They smashed through a fancy screen wall and slid down a steep slope of ice . . . just as the monastery exploded above them.

Ducard's limp body skidded down the frozen slope. He spun faster and faster toward the edge of the cliff.

Bruce dove across the ice and grabbed Ducard's arm. After a mighty struggle, Bruce stopped Ducard from falling down into the chasm.

Bruce carried Ducard to a sherpa's hut in the village.

"I will tell him you saved his life," said the old man.

"Tell him I had to go save a city," Bruce replied. He walked away and began his journey back to Gotham City.

It was time for Bruce Wayne to go home and face his fears. It was time to become the great warrior he had trained to be.

It was time to become Batman.